The Snowman Capers of Finneus Bleek

Kevin Watts

WestBow
PRESS
A DIVISION OF THOMAS NELSON

WestBow Press books may be ordered through booksellers or by contacting:

WestBow Press
A Division of Thomas Nelson
1663 Liberty Drive
Bloomington, IN 47403
www.westbowpress.com
1 (866) 928-1240

ISBN: 978-1-4908-1176-5 (sc)
ISBN: 978-1-4908-1177-2 (e)

Printed in the United States of America.

WestBow Press rev. date: 11/5/2013

CHAPTER 1

Here we go again

"Fin, supper!" shouted his mom from the kitchen. Fin didn't hear her. His mind was focused on building an electric garage door opener for his building block house. His mom got him the building block set from a garage sale for two dollars and the motor came from a toy that someone had thrown away in the trash.

"Imagine, someone throwing away this great stuff," Fin thought as he built his masterpiece.

The door creaked open.

"Finneus Bleek, your supper is ready. Please put your toys away and come to the table," mom insisted. Fin tidied his blocks and made his way into the narrow hallway. The door to his bedroom creaked, as it swung open. The hallway was nice and bright as new wallpaper was put up only six months ago. It was donated by some friends and had obviously been sitting around awhile. The glue on the back wasn't as sticky as it should be and some of the corners were already starting to peel away from the wall. The hall carpet was old and dingy. It looked greyer than it used to be when it was installed. There were also some stains that just wouldn't come clean anymore. Fin's mom did her best to keep it nice, but it was a lost cause.

In the living room, there was a picture of his grandpa Joe. Fin liked that it could be seen from his place at the kitchen table. Grandpa Joe had passed away a couple of months ago. In his will, he left Fin with two experimental science kits. One was all about motion and properties of physics. The other was an electrical building kit to make cool things like doorbells, working lights, gears, and more. There was also a note left to Fin by his grandpa Joe. It read:

Fin, I know you will do great things in your life, and these science kits will encourage you to find your path. Learn what you can from them to gain knowledge; but wisdom lies when you can apply that knowledge to your life. Remember though, wisdom isn't enough in itself either. Use the goodness inside you together with your wisdom to benefit others. That is when greatness is attained. Love always. Grandpa Joe.

Fin kept this letter on the shelf above his bed, as his grandpa's letter was very important to him.

Fin finally made his way into the kitchen. It was a very small space. The kitchen table was tucked into the corner of the room. No one could sit at one of the four available places at the table for it would block the oven door from opening. Fin wedged his way between the wall and the table and squeezed himself into the chair. Fried bologna and mashed potatoes stared back at him from his plate. He was getting tired of eating the same thing for it was the fourth time they had eaten it this week. Still, he was thankful not to go hungry.

"How come we aren't blessed like some other families?" Fin sputtered the words as he ate his mashed potatoes.

"We are blessed!" replied his dad. His dad Roger had a way about him that showed people he was sincere when he spoke. The corners of his mouth turned into a slight smile while the rest of his face beamed with joy. "We are able to work hard and are not relying on others to provide for our needs."

"Besides," his mom Carol interrupted, "we have a very bright and mannerly son who fills our house with joy. How's the new project coming along?"

Fin's mom and dad always seemed to know the right things to say to make him feel better. Roger worked at the local landfill site sorting the garbage. He would often find items that people would just throw away and bring them home for Fin to use in his designs. He always said the work was good even though it wasn't the greatest of pay. He believes the treasures he finds there make up the difference in pay. Fin's mom tries to make her own candles and sell them on the side. She wasn't very successful at this business, but she enjoyed what she did. She says that not everybody is blessed to do a job that they like as much as she enjoys hers.

Fin finished his meal and put his dishes in the sink.

"Thanks for supper mom." He sped back to his room eager to finish his work on the toy electric garage door opener. He was almost finished his prototype design and wanted to try it out before bedtime.

"There," beamed Fin, "that should do it." He hooked up the battery and the garage door of his building block house seemed to rise like magic. It wouldn't however go back down even if Fin switched the battery around. "I guess I'll have to change the cables around before it will work properly," thought Fin.

It wasn't long before his mom opened the door again.

"Fin, you had better get ready for bed. You need to be well rested for your first day of school this year." Fin reluctantly went to the bathroom to brush his teeth. He wanted to finish his project. Still, his mom was right. He needed the rest if he was going to perform his best tomorrow. Fin was looking forward to school this year. He had Mrs. Black for a teacher, who was known to be the best teacher at the school. He was eager to learn new and exciting things this year. There was one thing he was not very anxious about though; meeting up with Derek Malloy.

CHAPTER 2

First Day of School

Morning seemed to arrive like lightning. Fin jumped out of bed and ran to his cramped corner of the breakfast table.

"Morning mom. What's for breakfast?"

"Mashed potato pancakes," beamed his mom. It seems she had found a new way to use the leftovers from last night's meal. Fin's mom never wasted a single morsel of food. The pancakes tasted pretty good though, so Fin wasn't complaining.

Fin finished up and put his dishes in the sink. He made his way to the bathroom to make sure his brown hair was spiked up and his teeth were brushed. He wanted to look good for the first school day.

"Your lunch is in the bag on the table," said Fin's mom. "Don't forget your jacket." Fin stopped at the door so his mom could help him. She had made a very special jacket for him all by herself. It was made from all different types of materials sewn together. Fin's mom often

5

sang that song coat of many colors as she put it on him, and today was no different. "There. You're all set for grade three. You are getting so big." There was almost a tear in his mom's eyes as she spoke those words to him. "Don't forget to get Sarah on your way. She wants to walk with you to school."

"I won't mom," said Fin as he headed out for his first day of grade three. Fin walked in front of the neighbor's house and then stopped to scan the area. It seemed that Fin was in luck as there was no Derek Malloy to be found. Derek lived only two doors down from him in one of the nicer houses on the street. They always had everything looking so crisp and clean there. Derek was a bully in the neighborhood who seemed to have it out for Fin. He was huge too! From Fin's view, he looked like the size of an entire tree. Fin let out a big sigh of relief as he passed Derek's house to the next home where Sarah lived.

Sarah Windham was Fin's very best friend. She was smart too, but in a different way from Fin. Sarah had a very quick wit, where Fin was the inventive type. Together, they made a great team. Fin was excited that they were in the same class again this year. He couldn't wait to see her.

Fin sauntered up to the front door, not really paying too much attention. He was about to ring the doorbell, when all of a sudden he was taken by surprise. There was a loud rustling sound and a huge yell coming from the bush beside him.

"AAHHHHHHHH!" Fin jumped back in a hurry, fell backward off the front step and landed on his back on Sarah's front lawn. Teams of laughter came from the bush.

"You should have seen your face," giggled Sarah. "I knew you would be nervous about Derek, so I had to jump out at you." Sarah's blue eyes sparkled as she grinned at Fin. Her neck length hair peered out from under her winter hat and partially covered her right eye like it always did. Fin got up rubbing his backside and brushing the dead leaves off his coat.

"Yah, Real funny," he said shakily as he struggled to regain his composure.

"What are you trying to do, give me a heart attack?" Fin took a deep sigh of relief as he pushed his glasses back up on the bridge of his nose.

"Are you ready for another year at school?" Sarah was as excited as Fin was to start her first school day of the year.

"This will be the best year ever!" Fin beamed as they started out for the school.

The day was crisp and bright. You could smell the cleanliness in the air. Fin and Sarah got lost in their conversation and weren't really paying attention to what was up in front of them.

All of a sudden, Fin ran into what seemed to be a brick wall. He was looking at Sarah when he hit something. It was enough of a jolt to knock him down for the second time that morning. Fin looked up. It wasn't a wall he hit but it might as well have been. There looking back at Fin was the scariest thing he had ever seen. He had one thick furry eyebrow that curled downwards in the middle of it, and he had this sly, confident smirk, which made Fin feel he had no hope of getting away. This was the thing Fin feared the most. It was Derek Malloy.

CHAPTER 3

This Can't Be Happening!

"Well, well! If it isn't Finneus Geek and his little girlfriend Sarah Window," Derek beamed as he stood towering over Finneus's sprawled out body. It seemed like Derek's shadow covered the entire sidewalk. Sarah piped in.

"I might be the window, but you are the pane," she said in a frustrated voice. Derek glared over at Sarah with a scowl on his face but didn't comment. Then, he quickly turned back to Finneus and reached for his lunch bag.

"What have you got for lunch this year?" Derek was looking for any reason to give Fin a hard time about what little his family had.

"Baloney," Finneus replied in a weak and shaky voice.

"Can't your family afford anything else? You always eat the same thing everyday!" Derek pointed out. The smirk on his face showed that he believed he had the upper hand on this situation; and he did.

"I like baloney!" Finneus replied standing up for himself. Finneus was still thankful not to go hungry and it didn't matter to him it was baloney. Derek grabbed a hold of the baloney sandwich and squeezed it between his two massive palms. The sandwich was as flat as a pancake when he threw it back at Fin.

"Your sandwich seems to be a little flat. Maybe you should try using some spices next time." Derek walked away laughing to himself thinking he was so clever on how he handled Fin. Sarah helped Fin pick up his stuff.

"Derek makes me so mad," she verbalized with disgust.

"Why does he have to be so mean to you all the time Fin?"

They walked to school reasonably in silence the rest of the way. Fin tried very hard to stop thinking about the morning's incident but it seemed impossible to get it out of his mind. Sarah seemed to be still angry too. Fin was glad she was there to support him.

When they entered Mrs. Black's classroom, there was a buzz in the air. Everyone was talking about their summer holidays and all the neat experiences they had had. Fin didn't have much to say. He didn't have any travel experiences to share and not too many people shared his enthusiasm to invent and build things. He settled into a second row chair as Sarah sat at the desk beside him. Mrs. Black entered the room. She looked thrilled to see all her new students. She knew many of them from the hallways during the previous year.

Mrs. Black really looked like a teacher. She had long dark hair that was always pulled back and she wore glasses; the rectangle shaped ones that made her look very professional. She also wore similar type of clothing a business person would wear.

The first quarter of school seemed to go very fast. It seemed like no time until the bell rang for first nutrition break. Fin and Sarah decided they would go to the library on their break to see if there were any new books worth checking out this year.

On their way down the hall, Sarah noticed the same picture fastened to many of the lockers.

"What is this?" Sarah inquired as she pulled a picture off one of the locker doors. It was a picture of Fin sitting on the toilet. Fin looked at the picture in horror.

"That is not even my body!" Fin gasped. "Someone has pasted a picture of my head on this picture and photo shopped it with a computer."

Fin and Sarah looked around to see who might be the culprit. Derek was standing by the corner of the locker laughing at Fin.

"Didn't know I was that good with the computer, did you geek?" Derek chuckled. Fin's face glowed red with embarrassment as he glanced around to see the other students looking at his picture or pointing and laughing in his direction. Fin crumpled up the picture in his hand and threw it onto the ground. He and Sarah hurried towards the library so they could get away from the teams of laughter.

They entered the library and Fin let out a huge sigh. He looked over at Sarah with almost a tear in his eye. Sarah returned a slight smile and said, "Maybe you'll find some new books. That will cheer you up!"

Sarah was right. Looking at some new books would take his mind off the recent events in the hallway. Fin was thrilled to find some new books on mechanical inventions throughout history. Sarah got the new "Judy" novel. Fin checked out a tall stack of books. He could carry them all but it was hard to see over the top of the pile while he walked.

They started walking back down the hall where the embarrassing event happened. The laughter had subsided and Fin was somewhat relieved it didn't continue longer.

All of a sudden, Fin seemed to be shoved off balance and into the lockers. He toppled off the lockers onto the floor and the books were scattered everywhere. Derek had just walked by and was being his usual self. Fin could hear Derek laughing in the background at what he had done.

Fin scrambled to pick up the books. His face became increasingly red in color as his anger rose up. Sarah bent down to help.

"THAT'S IT!" Finneus yelled.

"I HAVE HAD ENOUGH. I AM NOT GOING THROUGH ANOTHER YEAR PUTTING UP WITH DEREK. THIS IS GOING TO STOP!"

"What can you do?" Sarah exclaimed. "He is so big and we are so small."

"He may be bigger than me, but I am way smarter than he is!" Finneus protested.

"I will get him back alright, only he is not gong to know who did it!" A mischievous grin perked up on Finneus as he started to dream up his devious plan.

CHAPTER 4

The Planning Begins

After school was over, Finneus left Sarah and went home. He threw open the door like a bull out of control. The noise startled his mom.

"How was your first day of school sweetie?" his mom asked eager to hear how he made out.

"Terrible," Fin yelled as he went into his room and slammed the door. It wasn't long before his mom knocked and opened the door.

"What happened that was so terrible?" his mom inquired.

"Derek always picks on me because I am small and different," Fin exclaimed, as his face grew red again.

"I don't want to go through another year of being picked on."

"Do you want me to speak to Derek's parents?" she asked with compassion for Fin's situation.

"No, that will only make things worse," Fin replied.

"I will have to look after this myself."

Fin's mom tried to change the subject to distract him.

"I see you got some new books from the library."

Fin looked over at the books. Then he got a brilliant idea on how to get back at Derek.

"THAT'S IT!" stated Fin.

"What's it?" asked his mom.

"Not right now mom. I have a new project to design," explained Fin.

Fin's mom just shrugged her shoulders and decided to go start on supper. Fin got out some paper and started to draft up some plans; something that would get Derek back.

"These plans are great! This will be perfect," Fin beamed as he finished the final touches. Fin's dad knocked on the open door.

"Your mom tells me you had a rough first day at school." Fin didn't really hear his dad speak.

"Dad, do you think you could get some supplies from the landfill site for my newest big project?" Fin asked excitedly. "Here is a list of the things I will need."

1. Chicken fence wire (a bunch)
2. 4 large door hinges
3. 8 metal dowel rods with 2 sleeves
4. Lots of white fabric
5. A bit of black fabric
6. A little bit of spandex material
7. 2 regular hinges and 2 ball and socket hinges.

"What are you building for this great project?" his dad asked quizzically.

"I need it to be a secret. You will find out pretty soon," replied Fin.

"Do you think you can get this stuff?"

"Yes, I think I can find all this stuff at work," Roger stated.

"I wish you would tell me what you are building." Fin just stared at his dad.

"Well, supper is ready, so please wash up and come to the table," Fin's dad said as he shrugged his shoulders and walked down the hall to the kitchen.

Fin made his way to the kitchen sink to wash up and squeezed his way into his normal seat at the table. While eating his mashed potato something or other his mind was thinking of how to build his new contraption. Every detail had to be perfect.

Fin's dad broke the silence.

"You know Fin when it comes to a person like Derek, there are two things you can do to improve your situation with him. The first one is to not let his bullying change you inside. Try not to let it bother you. The second is to try to do something nice for him. Who knows, he may actually become a good friend in the process. Then he will stop bullying you."

"He will soon not bully me anymore," Fin said with a revengeful look on his face.

"What are you going to do?" Fin's mom inquired, as she was concerned about the look on Fin's face when he said that.

"I just have to deal with this my own way," Fin stated as he cleaned up the plate in front of him.

Fin went back to his room to make the final modifications he thought of while he was eating supper.

"This would still be the best year yet," Fin said to himself, as he got ready for bed.

CHAPTER 5

The next Two Months In A Snap

Fin woke up in a great mood. He was pleased with himself about the plans he had made to get back at Derek. Fin got ready for school and went out to Sarah's to walk with her to school again. He was so deep in thought he didn't even scan the area for Derek as he sauntered past his house. Sarah was just coming out of her house as Fin turned onto her driveway. Fin had a huge smile on his face as Sarah approached him.

"You seem to be in a good mood considering all you went through yesterday," Sarah said with a pleased smirk on her face.

"Lets just say I have a foolproof plan on how to get Derek back for all the trouble he has caused me over the years," Fin embellished with a devious grin on his face.

"What are you going to do? Derek is not going to get hurt is he?" inquired Sarah.

"No. Lets just say that Derek won't be nearly as confident in himself when my plan has been put into action," Finneus announced. There was a moment of silence while each of them looked at each other. Sarah had a curious look on her face. She wanted to know Fin's plan. Fin was obviously not ready to share his plan yet so she had to be content for the time being.

Derek came racing by, knocking Fin onto the ground as he passed. Fin looked up to see Derek chuckling and pointing at Fin. Fin could feel the anger building up inside. Revengeful thoughts ran through his mind as he went over the plans in his mind. Sarah was more curious than ever as she watched Fin go through an array of emotion she had never witnessed in him before. They finished their walk to school in silence.

The next couple of months seemed to go by very fast. Fin spent every spare minute he could on building his masterpiece. Derek was still his usual self, bothering Finneus every chance he got. Sarah felt she was left out for a while because Finneus' thoughts were focused on his project rather than spending quality time with her. Sarah finally confronted Fin.

"I have missed spending the time we used to spend together Fin! It seems all you can focus on is your project." Sarah felt hurt as she struggled to get the words out.

"I am almost finished," Fin said beaming with pride. "Then Derek will get what he deserves. All I have to do now is put the finishing touches on it and wait for it to snow."

"You have been so secretive about this whole thing. What is it you are making?" Sarah inquired.

"You have to keep it secret," Fin whispered to Sarah. "If anyone ever found out and it got back to Derek, I would not live to see another day. The only way this will work is if no one else knows anything about it; ever."

"I promise I won't tell anyone," Sarah replied with curiosity.

"It's a mechanical snowman which I can control from the inside of it," Fin announced.

"What good is that going to do?" Sarah wondered out loud.

"Derek will think he is losing his mind as a snowman starts doing things to him that seem to be impossible," Fin gloated.

Sarah winked and the two of them set out to discuss the possibilities that might happen to Derek as time goes on.

After school, Fin made the finishing touches required to make his snowman complete. He was extremely pleased with his accomplishment.

"This plan is wicked!" Fin thought to himself as he put on the last piece of fabric. "Now, if it would only snow." Just then, there was a knock on the door.

"Fin, can I come in?" his dad said from the hallway.

"Sure dad," Fin replied. "You gotta see my project. I am all done."

Roger opened the door and peered inside the room not knowing what to expect. He knew how upset Fin was about Derek being a bully to him for a while. Roger was relieved to see a snowman staring back at him.

"Well, that's a fine looking snowman," Roger beamed with pride. "Why was this such a secret?"

"This is the key to make Derek stop bullying me," Fin said with relief in his voice. Fin's dad looked concerned.

"No one is going to get hurt, are they Fin?" his dad asked with a concerned voice.

"Nothing outside of a snowball hitting him," Fin exclaimed pride fully. "Here dad. Let me show you how it works." Fin opened up the back hatch and climbed in. He grabbed onto the controls on the inside and started working them with extreme skill. He was able to make the snowman bend down and pick up a medium sized rubber ball off the floor of his room. Then Fin launched the ball across the room with the snowman and hit a target he had set up for practice.

"That is amazing!" Fin's dad said with excitement in his voice; but he was still concerned. "You have done a great job. This is your best invention yet. I am concerned about the motivation behind your design though Fin. It is never a good thing to act on revenge over an incident. God says we should love our enemies and pray for them."

"This isn't about revenge dad," Fin explained. It seems like Derek has bullied me all my life. I just want the bullying to stop so I can try to live a normal life."

"That's just it Fin; you aren't normal. You are special and you have special gifts," his dad said with a smile.

"I do feel that I can accomplish great things dad," Fin said. But, as long as Derek keeps bullying me, he will always keep me distracted from my inventions. I don't want my potential to be clouded so I can accomplish great things just like Grandpa Joe said in his letter."

"Grandpa Joe's letter said that you would attain greatness when you use the goodness inside you to help people, not your knowledge for revenge," Roger said with disappointment in his voice. Fin didn't really hear that statement. He busied himself with his mechanical snowman and was dazed in his thoughts. Roger let out a big sigh and started to leave the room.

"Oh by the way," Fin's dad said as he turned around. "Supper is ready, and you might be able to use your snowman sooner than you think. It is starting to snow."

CHAPTER 6

Here Goes Nothing!
The Moment of Truth

Fin finished off his supper in a hurry and raced to his room. Gathering up all his snowman gear he dragged it to the front door.

"Don't forget to put on your hat and mitts," Fin's mom called to him as he raced to get ready. Fin headed out to find the perfect spot for his creation. He wanted it to be close enough to the sidewalk that he could get a good shot at Derek, but far enough away so that Derek would have to take good aim to get his snowman with a snowball. All of Fin's practicing would finally pay off. The snow was coming down hard as Fin worked diligently trying to get his snowman packed with snow so it blended in with the front yard and not look suspicious. It was perfect. Fin hopped into the back of the snowman to give it a test run.

Fin's dad watched out the window as Fin worked vigorously. He was worried that Fin's motivation behind his snowman creation was not as pure as it should be. Still, if no one would get hurt, then he guessed he would just have to pray for a positive result and let Finneus make his own choice.

The test run of the snowman went great. It seemed to be working very well. The last thing Fin had to do was to move piles of snow close to him so that he could reach it from inside the snowman. About twenty minutes of shoveling and Fin was ready. He stood there and marveled at his creation. Pleased with his results, Fin said to himself,

"Derek won't know what hit him."

Fin went inside and started getting ready for bed. His dad caught his attention.

"Are you sure you are doing the right thing?" Roger asked with a concerned overtone in his voice.

"Yes, dad. I'm sure." Fin reassured his dad. "This is the only way I know how to get Derek to stop picking on me."

His dad swallowed hard.

"Just keep me posted on the progress," replied his dad as he left the room to go and pray for his son. It was hard to let his son solve this large of a problem on his own, but he thought this would be a good teaching lesson for Fin as long as no one got hurt.

Finneus had a difficult time getting to sleep that night. He tossed and turned thinking about all the different scenarios that might happen in the morning with the throw of the first snowball. Fin knew that Derek always made it a tradition of his to throw at least one snowball at him on the first snow of the season. Fin really didn't understand why Derek felt it necessary to do that, but that was what he did. He expected this year would be no different. This would be the perfect opportunity to get the upper hand on Derek for the first time ever.

Not all the scenarios that Fin thought of went off perfectly, but the one thing his mind kept coming back to was the fact that Derek would get what's coming to him. That was enough for him to try. Still, in the back of his mind, he kept thinking about what his dad said about doing something nice for Derek.

"Nah, that would be useless when it comes to Derek," Fin thought as he tried to reason his motivation for the snowman. "This is the only way."

After awhile he drifted off to sleep. Morning would come soon. This was going to be a monumental day.

CHAPTER 7

Flight of the Snowball

Early morning came and Fin was up, raring to get everything set for the first snowball. He knew he would have to be out there early if he wanted to beat Derek to the punch of getting the first snowball in the air. Fin was even up before his mom and dad were. He decided that oatmeal was the thing to have this morning. After all, it was a special occasion. He made enough for his mom and dad too. Even though he was focused on his snowman and Derek, his mom and dad were still very important to him, so he wanted to help them too.

By the time his mom got out of bed, Fin had the breakfast made and had just finished eating.

"Wow, look at this. What is the occasion?" Fin's mom beamed.

"We are celebrating the first day I can try out my new invention," Fin replied excitedly. His mom's face showed a bit of discontent as Fin stated the reason for his excitement.

"Don't worry mom. It will be great!" Fin exclaimed as he tidied up his dishes and started to get ready to go outside.

"Make sure you bundle up," his mom said to Fin as she always did. "I will get your school lunch ready."

"Whatever you do, don't come outside to get me. I will be in later to get my lunch. I can't afford to have my cover blown after all this time of preparing," Fin stated in a very serious tone.

His mom raised her one eyebrow as she watched Fin close the door behind him. Carol couldn't stop wondering what would become of this chain of events. It seemed that all she could do now was to hope and pray that no one would get hurt and that maybe Fin and Derek could find a way to get along.

Fin arrived at his snowman in the front yard and decided it would be a good idea to give it a test run. He went to the spot where he figured Derek would be and set up a target to shoot at. With target set Fin climbed into the snowman and got comfortable in his seat. He reached for the controls and did some test movements. Side to side, back and forth, and turning the body were a little stiff from the cold but became looser as he moved them around. Now it was time to check the arms and throwing mechanism. Fin turned and bent the snowman body to reach the pile of snow he piled beside the snowman the night before. He used the snowman arms to pick up some snow and pack it into a ball. The snowman's arm came back and launched a speedy and accurate shot. Right on target!

"Derek won't know what hit him," he said to himself as he got out of the snowman to go clean up the target. Fin didn't want there to be any evidence there was a plan going on so that Derek wouldn't be any wiser.

Fin ran back inside for a very brief moment to get his lunch from his mom.

"Thanks for my lunch mom and remember, don't come outside in case you spoil my plan," Fin said as he grabbed it and took his backpack outside to hide it in the bushes. He did this so his mom didn't feel tempted to come outside at just the wrong moment and ruin everything.

All there was to do now was to wait for Derek. Fin sat down inside the snowman and got comfortable. At first, it seemed to go by pretty fast as the anticipation of this great event got the best of him, but as the time slipped on, Fin started to get tired from being up so early that morning. Then Fin remembered he had better get a snowball ready in the snowman's hand. He wanted to be ready when Derek came past so he wouldn't make any sudden movements to alert his target.

It wasn't long after that he saw Derek sauntering down the street towards his house. Fin knew that Derek was predictable enough that he would go out of his way to throw a snowball at something, or someone, at his place. Fin got really nervous and excited all at once as Derek approached closer to the house. Fin was ready. He stayed perfectly still as he watched Derek scan the area to see what would be a good target for him. Derek focused on the snowman with the intent to have his thrown snowball knock the head off the snowman.

Derek bent down to get some snow packed into a snowball. This was Fin's chance to make his throw. The snowman's arm came back and let off a blistering launch.

WHAM-MO! It was a direct hit on the side of Derek's head so hard that it knocked him off balance and he lost the snow in his hands. The cold snow started to melt right away down the side of his face and into his jacket. It was cold and uncomfortable. Derek was upset.

"WHO DID THAT?" Derek yelled as he glanced around the yard to find evidence of someone to go after. Fin stayed as still as possible inside the snowman. His heart was pounding. He seemed to be paralyzed with anxiousness. Derek looked as mean as ever. He went to reach down to grab another snowball. This was Fin's chance to get another snowball and go for the throw. Fin reached down quickly and picked up the snowball he had made yesterday and launched a thunderous throw.

Derek thought he caught some motion out of the corner of his eye, and looked up. The snowball was already well on its way to him. Derek didn't have enough time to react.

WHACK! Derek got one right on the forehead with enough force it took his hat off. Derek was furious.

"Whoever did this is done for," Derek whined as he approached where the snowman was. Fin felt as if his heart stopped beating. Derek was close and if he were caught, this would be the end of Fin. Luckily for Fin though, Derek was so focused on finding the culprit for his snowball incident, he forgot all about wrecking the snowman. His search led him around the snowman, over by the big maple tree in the front yard, around the corner of the house and back.

Derek had no luck. He couldn't find anyone to blame for his misery. He stood beside the snowman steaming with anger. Fin could almost feel the heat off of Derek as his blood pressure raised. He kept scanning the area as he reached over to the snowman and pulled the carrot nose off of the snowman.

"**I will be back and you will pay for this,**" Derek yelled as he began to leave, munching on the carrot nose he had just picked.

"Imagine that," Fin thought in his head.

"Derek just picked the snowman's nose and ate it."

Fin let out a chuckle and a big sigh of relief as he was finally left alone. The coast was clear as Fin climbed out of the snowman and made his way to Sarah's house to walk with her to school. His heart was still pounding as they began to discuss the events of the morning.

"Weren't you afraid?" Sarah inquired as she looked intently at Fin to see his facial expressions.

"Man, my heart was pounding like crazy!" Fin exclaimed as they made their way to the school. They saw Derek up ahead of them but he seemed to be lost in his thoughts and didn't pay any attention to Fin and Sarah.

"Wow, this is the first day since the beginning of school that Derek hasn't gone out of his way to do something mean to you," Sarah said.

"Yeah. It appears that my plan is working already," Fin beamed as they made their way to class.

CHAPTER 8

I'm Done For!

School went by quickly again today. Fin and Sarah were walking home together discussing the one event that was stranger than any other day this year.

"You have gone the whole day without Derek bothering you once Fin," Sarah said as her breath made clouds in the air from the cold.

"I know. This seems very strange," Fin replied with a mildly excited expression. "Hopefully, my plan has started to work. I'm getting tired of being bullied everyday."

Fin spoke too soon. All of a sudden, Fin caught something out of the corner of his eye. He turned to look to the side when, **SPLUT!**

A snowball hit Fin right on the head. Teams of laughter came from the huge wall known as Derek Malloy.

"What did you do that for?" Fin said with a frustrated and surprised voice. Derek could hardly contain his amusement.

"I'm just getting into the right frame of mind to watch my movie tonight," Derek gleamed. "It is called **THE ATTACK OF THE SNOWMEN FROM MARS.**"

Derek laughed as he walked away from Fin and Sarah. Fin let out a big, frustrated sigh. The snow started to melt down the side of his face. It was cold and uncomfortable. Fin wiped it away as best as he could.

"I guess we didn't make as much progress as we thought," Fin grumbled as they sauntered home. "I will keep at it though. I still believe this is the right approach to get Derek to stop bugging me."

They arrived outside Sarah's house.

"See you tomorrow Fin," Sarah said with compassion for her friend. She really wants Fin to succeed on his plan; and not get killed by Derek.

"Bye Sarah," Fin replied as he went home to analyze his snowman to see if any modifications could be made.

Fin went through the chain of events over and over in his mind from this morning. He remembered that Derek had gone around the back of the snowman at one point. He realized that if Derek had taken the thought to knock the head off the snowman, Fin's head would have been taken off too. He needed to make a couple of holes in the back so he could see all around in case he had to duck and save his neck.

Fin went inside when he got home and took another carrot out of the fridge to replace the nose that Derek had taken that morning. After fixing the snowman's carrot nose, Fin quickly started to make a couple of holes in the back of its' head so he could peer through them. He also needed to make sure there was some snowball ammunition ready for him to grab in a hurry when Derek came by tomorrow.

Fin finished up and went inside. He took off his wet outer clothes and hung them up to dry by the space heater they used to heat the main room. He made his way to the cramped side of the table to complete his homework when his mom entered the kitchen.

"How was your day today Fin?" his mom asked with relief that her boy wasn't injured from the events of the day. She watched the whole thing out the window that morning.

"It wasn't too bad," Fin replied while deep in thought about the upcoming events in the morning. "I still have a ways to go to reach my goal."

Fin finished the math with ease and enjoyed his fried bologna and mashed potato supper. He made his way to his room and saw his building block house with the prototype of the electric garage door opener still unfinished. Fin thought he needed a distraction from the recent events and decided to rework the cables on the garage door. Running some small pulleys around the back of the garage and hooking up the cables in the right direction seemed to do the trick. It was amazing how much Fin had learned about design just by building his snowman. The motorized garage door opener intrigued Fin. Maybe his snowman creation could be motorized too. It was getting late so Fin brushed his teeth and went to bed. His mom tucked him in and gave him a kiss goodnight. She said how proud she was to have a great little boy in the house like Fin. She always said that but Fin never got tired of hearing it. He was very tired after an extremely long and intense day so it wasn't long before he drifted off to sleep.

Morning came and Fin was up a little later than the previous day. He had to hurry and eat so he could get his spot in the snowman before Derek came by again.

"Mom, please do not come outside and spoil my cover again this morning. It is really important that I stay hidden," Fin reasoned with his mom.

His mom reluctantly agreed and Fin took off out the door with his backpack. This time, he decided to put his backpack inside the snowman with him so as not to leave any clue to who was throwing the snowballs.

Fin climbed into the snowman and got settled with a snowball in hand just in time before Derek came trudging up the street. Fin knew he would be here again after yesterday's loss. Derek was scanning the area to see if the culprit from yesterday was there to throw another snowball. All he could see was the snowman. Derek bent down to gather up some snow as Fin launched another thunderous throw.

Derek caught the motion out of the corner of his eye and became suspicious. He was too slow to move out of the way as the snowball caught him on the front of his coat. Derek's eyes narrowed.

"I could have swore that snowman threw the snowball at me," Derek said quietly to himself. He stared at the snowman for a minute then shook his head.

"My mind must be playing tricks on me from the snowman movie I watched last night. I still got hit by a snowball though," Derek said to himself as his suspicious eyes squinted again.

Derek slowly crept towards the snowman. His eyes narrowed, and stayed fixed where Fin was hiding. Fin's heart felt like it nearly dropped to his feet. Fin was paralyzed with fear. All he could do was to wait and pray. Derek inched closer and closer. His eyes fixed on the snowman's eyes. Closer and closer he got till his nose was touching the carrot. Fin could almost feel his breath through the snowman's eyeholes, which were covered with spandex material. It was like the snowman and Derek were having a staring contest. Neither one blinked.

Fin thought to himself, "I am a goner for sure."

CHAPTER 9

A Goner For Sure

Derek was squinting hard into the snowman's eyes. Fin could see the vein popping out on his forehead. He felt like fleeing but he had to say still, practically helpless. Derek stared intensely at the snowman, which seemed like an hour. There was no hope. Fin thought he was about to get pounded. He was about to try to run away but he was frozen with fear and felt like he couldn't breathe.

All of a sudden, Derek's eyes opened up from his squinting and he made a smacking motion on his head while saying to himself.

"I must be going crazy. Snowmen can't move. I've got to stop watching those scary movies. It is making my mind play tricks on me."

Derek started to walk away while mumbling to himself. He made his way down the road to school as he always did. It looked like he was having a conversation with himself as he walked. Fin thought maybe he was already crazy.

Once it was safe, Fin got out of the back of the snowman and grabbed his backpack. His body was still shaking from all the adrenaline pumping through his blood. By the time he got to Sarah's house, he was still pretty shaky. Sarah came out to meet him.

"What happened?" Sarah inquired. "You look like a wreck and you're shaking like crazy."

Fin proceeded to tell Sarah about the events of that morning.

"I thought I would be killed for sure," Fin exclaimed. "Derek thought he saw the snowman move and came right up to it and stared me straight in the eyes. I thought my plan was spoiled for sure and I would be dead. But then Derek said he has to stop watching those scary snowmen movies because it is making his mind play tricks on him and then he just walked away."

"No wonder you are shaking," Sarah responded. "I would be scared out of my mind."

"That scary snowman movie that Derek watched last night is the only thing that stopped me from being pounded," Fin said with a sigh of relief.

"It is time for me to step the snowman design up to the next level. It has to be motorized if I am going to have a chance at scaring Derek and make him think he has lost his mind."

"It might be a good idea to try to make a snowman mask peek out around corners at him so that he really thinks his mind has left him," Sarah said excitedly as she thought she had a brilliant plan.

"That is a great idea Sarah," Fin announced excitedly. "This will surely put him over the edge. I am going home tonight to install a motor on my snowman and make sure the snowman has angry eyebrows on it. Do you think you could make a snowman mask?"

"No problem, Fin," Sarah replied. I will have it done by the end of the weekend. "Between the two of us, we should be successful."

Fin drew up some plans at recess for Sarah's mask design. It had to be large enough to look real but small enough to be able to fit into Sarah's backpack. He gave them to her on the way home.

"You need to make this look as real as possible," Fin said. "Otherwise, Derek will be sure to find out our plan."

Fin and Sarah parted ways to work on their tasks for the weekend. It was Friday and Fin knew that Derek's family was going away for the next two days so this was perfect timing to modify his snowman.

Fin decided to go to his dad's work at the landfill site. His dad was there sorting scrap.

"Hi dad," Fin interrupted as his dad was talking to a coworker.

"Hi son. What are you doing here?" his dad inquired.

"I need some parts to modify my snowman design. Have you seen any of those vehicles that kids drive around?" asked Fin confidently. "A tank shaped one would be best so that it would go through the snow."

"How about a kids snowmobile," Fin's dad inquired. "You could use the track and frame off that. I know of an electric DC motor and a good battery that will hook right up to it as well."

"That would be great Dad," Fin raised his voice with excitement. "Do you think you could help me with the design this weekend? We could do those father, son things you have been asking about lately."

A little smile came at the corners of Rogers' mouth.

"I think that would be a great idea Fin," Roger replied with a little tear starting to form in his right eye. "It has been awhile since we have had this kind of quality time together. We will start on it tonight after supper. I will bring home the supplies."

"I am also going to need a three way toggle switch, a variable resistor to hook up to a pedal, and some wire," Fin added as his mind was racing to complete the design in his head.

"No problem," his dad said. "I can get all that stuff here. I will bring it home tonight."

"Thanks Dad," replied Fin as he left to go home and start working on the plans for the final design of the snowman.

"This will be amazing," Fin said to himself as he finished drawing his design. He had a looked at the parts his dad was going to bring home, so he had a rough idea of their capabilities. Fin felt he was smart enough to make it work with his dad's help.

His dad arrived home with a cart full of supplies from the landfill site where he worked. He had to borrow the cart from work to get all the parts home that Fin and him needed to complete the design. Fin was excited to get going on their creation.

"We can start on it right after supper," his dad offered. He could see the excitement in his son's eyes.

Fin's mom had supper ready when Roger arrived home. They were ready to eat and eager to get started on the design.

"I need to be able to go frontwards and backwards in the snowman. Do you think we can get the snowman to travel as fast as I can run?" Fin inquired with anticipation.

"Yes, I think this little snowmobile I brought home is supposed to get speeds up to 25 km/h," his dad replied. Roger was getting excited to work along side of his son. He knew how much his son loved building things from practically nothing.

They finished supper quickly and piled their dishes in the kitchen. Carol said she would look after cleaning the dishes if the boys wanted to get started on their big project.

"Do you think we have everything we need dad?" Beamed Fin.

"Yes, I think we are ready," replied his father. "Let's go."

CHAPTER 10

The Grand Design

Fin and his dad examined the snowmobile first. They decided that the track should be kept intact but the whole front end should be removed and moved closer to the track. That way, it would fit inside the snowman. The snowmobile was the perfect thing to use, as there was a battery compartment under the seat where Fin knew the battery would have to go in his design.

"That's about all we will do tonight Fin," his dad said with an exhausted sigh. "I'm tired from a long day at work. We can pick this up in the morning. I will borrow a welder from Sarah's dad in the morning so we can modify the frame of the snowmobile and attach it to the snowman frame."

Fin washed up to get rid of the grease on his hands from the snowmobile and got ready for bed. Fin hoped he could actually fall asleep as his mind was racing with the buzz of the build.

"Tomorrow should be enough time to complete the design," Fin thought to himself. "Maybe I will be able to do a test run too." It didn't take long until Fin fell asleep.

Morning came and Fin was up early. He bustled about trying to get things ready for breakfast when his dad came into the kitchen looking half asleep still.

"Anxious to keep building your project are you?" Roger said hardly able to keep his eyes open.

"Yah Dad. Are you ready to get started?" Fin inquired.

"Not without coffee, breakfast, and changing into my day clothes," Roger replied with a little smirk on his face. The fact that Fin was up so early was not a surprise to him. He knew his son well.

They finished their breakfast and Roger got ready for the fun day he and his son were going to have. Fin busied himself dry fitting the parts for the electric motor arm. Fin's dad had grabbed an adjustable arm from a car alternator at the landfill site. That is what they would use to adjust the tension on the belt for the drive of the snowmobile track. Some brackets would have to be welded to support the motor, the toggle switch and the steering mechanism. The toggle switch needed to be wired between the battery and the motor to control forward and backwards motion of the snowman. Roger came into the shed where they were working on their masterpiece.

"Do you think you have everything figured out Fin?" his dad asked while presenting a little yawn in the process.

"Yes, I think so dad," Fin replied. "We are going to need welds placed here for the toggle switch, and two here for mounting the motor. We are also going to have to put brackets all around the drive frame so I can attach my snowman shell to it. We will also need to reinforce the snowman shell so it doesn't buckle under the sudden change in direction. Do you think you could help me with all that?" The excitement in Fin's eyes couldn't be contained. His dad nodded with a smile.

"We had better get started then Fin," stated his dad. "Let's see if we can borrow the welder from Sarah's dad."

They both walked down to Sarah's house to ask Mr. Windham if they could borrow his welder. He was happy to lend it to them for the day but warned them to be careful with it. It could easily burn them.

"I use these tools at work," said Roger.

"Thanks for your concern, but you don't need to worry."

Sarah asked if she could come over to watch and maybe lend a hand with the project. Fin was happy to have her company and help.

They got back to the house and started right away. Fin's dad was good with the welder. Grandpa Joe taught his dad the safe and accurate way to use it. It only took about four hours to get to the point where they were ready to install it onto the snowman shell. The skis were cut to half the length and mounted close to the motorized track so it was compact enough to fit inside the snowman shell. The steering seemed to work flawlessly. Fin gave it a test run before they decided to put the final shell on the motor. Sarah tried it too. She squealed with excitement as she drove around the yard.

It was ready to go so Fin tied some extra cross braces inside the snowman shell for support. The snowman shell fit just right. It hovered above the level of the ground by a few inches and the tips of the skis stuck out the front by just a bit to allow for turning.

The three stood there and marveled at their accomplishment. This was quite a feat they took on and they were successful at their design. Fin turned to Sarah.

"How is the mask coming along?" Fin inquired. "Are you able to make it look really close to the face on this one?"

"I am almost done," Sarah responded. "It looks almost identical to this one too. I had better get home and finish working on it."

Sarah left for home while Fin and his dad cleaned up, and put the battery on the charger. Then they moved the snowman back into position ready for Monday.

"I'm thrilled we got the snowman done today," said Roger. "Tomorrow is meant to be our day of rest."

Fin agreed as he got some snowballs ready and cleaned up the tracks made from the snowmobile. Everything was ready for Monday. Derek would get the surprise of his life. This would surely put him over the edge. Fin could hardly wait.

CHAPTER 11

The Plan Worked Wonders

This was it; the day he was waiting for. This was the day that Derek would finally stop bullying him. It was Monday and Fin was up early as usual to get things ready for the encounter with Derek again. Fin's heart was racing with anticipation and nervousness. He wafted down his breakfast and went to check on the batteries for the snowman. They were fully charged and ready to go. Fin got them off the charger and took them to the front door. He was busy getting his boots on when his dad walked in.

"This is the big day, right Fin?" his dad asked. There wasn't much enthusiasm in his voice for he wasn't convinced that this plan of Fin's was the best way to handle his troubles with Derek. He helped his son build the snowman because he wanted Fin to know that he was loved no matter if he made the best choices or not. Roger just prayed that the outcome of this adventure didn't cause any further damage in the long run.

"Yes, dad. I think everything is ready to go," Fin replied with a faint sigh of relief in his voice.

"I need to do a quick test run before the event." Fin went outside with the battery in hand.

It was a brisk, clear day this morning. Fin could faintly see his breath as his warm breath hit the cold outside temperature. He worked diligently to get the snowman ready for the encounter with Derek. Fin got inside and started it up. He drove the snowman around a little bit getting it up to full speed. Everything was working perfectly. Fin parked the snowman in its home spot and went to make sure he covered up all the tracks he made during the test run. He also made sure there were a few snowballs ready to throw as Derek came up.

Fin just finished his preparation as he saw Derek just coming out his front door.

"Oh no, Derek's early," Fin said as he hurried to get into the back of the snowman. He didn't really feel mentally prepared. He didn't have time to just sit and wait in the snowman.

Derek scanned the area looking for any traces of someone who would throw snowballs. He eyed the snowman intently. Finneus stayed perfectly still. His heart was pounding in his chest. The moment he had been working towards was finally here. This is the moment of truth.

Derek stopped in front of the house where he normally did. He took one last scan of the area to see if he noticed anyone around. There was nothing to see. He bent down to make a snowball. Finneus launched a snowball with the snowman arm at the same time Derek looked up. The snowball came hurling towards Derek, but he was too quick this time. Derek moved out of the way of the speedy snowball and this time he was pretty sure it was the snowman that threw it.

Derek inched towards the snowman. He had a bit of a confused and concerned look on his face. Finneus saw the concerned look and decided this would be the only chance he had to move the snowman.

He prayed that Derek still remembered the snowman from Mars movie he watched last week. That would give him a fighting chance.

Derek was about half way to the snowman spot. He was moving very slowly. It was now or never. Fin had to move. He rose up the snowman arms quickly and let out a very loud yell as he pushed the lever forward to make the snowman rush towards Derek.

Derek was so scared he nearly jumped out of his clothes. He turned around tripping over himself and falling. He picked himself up and ran away screaming. He ran all the way to school without looking back to see if the snowman was still behind him.

Finneus laughed as he saw Derek running away. His plan was working really well. Derek would surely wonder about his sanity now after experiencing the events of the morning.

Fin parked the snowman and cleaned up the tracks he had made. He made his way down to Sarah's house. Sarah came out to meet him.

"I heard the screaming and looked out the window to see Derek running past the house at super speed," said Sarah with a small grin on her face.

"What happened?"

"Derek was scared out of his mind when I raced the snowman towards him," Fin replied while his face was beaming.

"Are we ready for phase two of the operation?"

"Yes, I have the snowman mask right here. What do you think of it?" Sarah asked with curiosity. She brought out the mask to show Fin.

"It looks perfect; just like my snowman," Fin beamed.

"This will put Derek over the edge for sure."

Sarah put the snowman mask in her backpack as they walked to school together. They could hardly contain their excitement over the events that would happen later today.

First period seemed to take forever to pass. They were eager to try out the mask on Derek during recess.

The bell rang so Sarah and Finneus went out to find out where Derek was hanging out with his friends. They saw him over by the monkey bars. He looked at little concerned. It seemed as if he was talking about the snowman scare he had that morning. His friends all had a smirk on their face while he was telling the story. Obviously, they did not believe him.

"I will run around the building and go past Derek from the other side towards you while you put on the snowman mask and peek around the corner. Hopefully while running past him, Derek will look over this way and notice the snowman head sticking out. We will have to stay separated so this can work. I don't want to run the risk that Derek can tie the snowman directly to me," Finneus said with anticipation.

Finneus took off around the other side of the building while Sarah put on the mask. Everything was in place. Sarah peeked out around the corner of the school building while Finneus ran past Derek making "Woo-Ho" noises and running about fifty feet to the right of where Sarah was peeking out with the snowman mask on.

The distraction worked. Derek looked up at Finneus and watched him run away. Then he noticed a strangely familiar looking snowman face from this morning peeking out at him from the corner of the building. A chill ran down Derek's spine. His eyes widened and his jaw dropped. The angry eyebrows that Sarah had put on it were a really nice touch. Sarah ducked in behind the corner, took the mask off and put it in her backpack as soon as Derek had enough of a look. She started to walk away trying not to grin.

"DID YOU SEE THAT," Derek sputtered as he poked his friends to get their attention. Derek pointed over to the corner of the building to where the snowman face was but his friends couldn't see anything.

"THAT SNOWMAN IS STALKING ME. COME WITH ME AND I'LL PROVE IT TO YOU," Derek exclaimed to his friends.

Derek dragged his friends around the corner to see if they could see the snowman. By this time, Sarah was a long way off in the distance among the other kids playing in the schoolyard. Derek's friends started laughing.

"I think you have lost your mind," his friends all chanted.

Derek ran up to numerous kids in the playground.

"Did you see a snowman over in the corner of the school?" Derek pleaded to the kids so he would know he wasn't crazy.

No one had seen it. At this time Derek was sure he had lost his mind. He noticed he was also not in control of his group of friends anymore for they all thought he was going crazy.

Sarah and Fin met up at the other side of the playground.

"How did it go?" Finneus inquired.

"Derek has completely lost his mind," said Sarah beaming.

"Our job is complete."

The rest of the day went easy. Derek was too preoccupied with the snowman events to worry about bullying anyone. This was a great victory.

CHAPTER 12

Life is Blissful

It was Friday already and Finneus was in the greatest of moods. Derek hadn't bullied him the whole week. Sarah and Fin made sure that Derek saw a snowman in his sight at least once a day all week. They either built a snowman in the schoolyard, or Sarah put on the mask and peeked around the corner at Derek.

Finneus was walking to school with Sarah in the morning as he always did when they noticed Derek off in the distance. He seemed to be very fidgety and was mumbling words to himself. It appeared that he was playing the snowman events over and over in his mind trying to make sense out of it all. Sarah and Fin walked past Derek.

"Good morning Derek," Fin beamed with a big smile on his face.

Derek didn't hear him. He was too busy mumbling to himself to pick up on what was going on around him. Fin looked at Sarah and gave a little smirk.

They got to school and sat in their usual places.

"Derek has really lost his mind," Sarah chirped.

"Do you think we pushed him too far?"

"NO!" warned Finneus.

"With the amount of bullying he has given me over the years, he deserves everything he gets."

Sarah shrugged her shoulders and they went back to their schoolwork. Recess was coming soon and they wanted to get finished their art project before they went outside.

The bell rang and everyone went outside to play. Fin and Sarah were having a good time on the monkey bars when Fin noticed something out of the corner of his eye. He stopped to take a look. There was Derek, sitting all by himself, rocking back and forth as he had been doing for the past few days. His friends seemed to have abandoned him and were playing ball in the field. For a moment, Fin had a touch of compassion for Derek. Derek's world had been changed upside down and it was all because of Fin's prank.

"He deserves it," Fin said again to himself hoping to alleviate his guilty conscience. Still, Fin couldn't get that lonely image of Derek out of his head. As the day went on Fin became angrier with himself wondering why he had compassion for Derek's condition all of a sudden. He was really frustrated with himself by the end of the day.

"How can a day start out so happy and end in frustration?" Fin wondered to himself. He went home still convincing his brain that he did the right thing by playing this prank on Derek.

He entered the house door and went straight to his room. Fin's mom peeked in.

"How was your day today Fin?" his mom inquired.

"I don't want to talk about it right now," replied Finneus.

"Maybe we can discuss it as a family when dad gets home."

Fin's mom was curious but closed the door and went to the kitchen to start supper.

Fin laid down on the bed and reached up to the shelf above the headboard to get the letter from Grandpa Joe. He opened up the letter and read it again like he did almost every night. Fin stared into the letter as if his Grandpa Joe was right there giving him some insight to his predicament.

Fin, I know you will do great things in your life, and these science kits will encourage you to find your path. Learn what you can from them to gain knowledge; but wisdom lies when you can apply that knowledge to your life. Remember though, wisdom isn't enough in itself either. Use the goodness inside you together with your wisdom to benefit others. That is when greatness is attained. Love always. Grandpa Joe.

"I have done some great things already Grandpa," Fin spoke into the air to his Grandpa's spirit.

"I have made some incredible inventions and have gained much knowledge. I know that you said I need to use the goodness inside me to become great but sometimes you just have to be selfish."

Fin put the letter back in the envelope and placed it on his chest while he laid in bed thinking about all the feelings he was going through. Fin could hear his mom and dad in the kitchen talking about the discussion that would take place at the dinner table with Fin.

His dad poked his head into the room.

"Supper is ready Fin. You can wash up and come to the table."

Roger closed the door again and went to wash up for dinner.

Fin dragged himself out of the bed and headed towards the bathroom to wash up. He passed his dad in the hall on the way but never made eye contact or said a word. Fin washed his hands and made his way to the table where he always sat. There was a long silence at the dinner table at first and then Fin spoke up.

"After Sarah and I played the prank on Derek, he has stopped bullying me. I thought I was feeling relieved and happy about this but, when I saw Derek today, he didn't seem himself. Instead of hanging around with his friends and joking, he was just sitting on his own at the corner of the school mumbling to himself. I couldn't help but to feel sorry for him. Why would I feel sorry for someone who has treated me so badly?" Fin spoke with disappointment in his voice.

Fin's mom smiled.

"If we are truly going to make a difference in someone's life then we are required to love them no matter what kind of things they do to us," Carol empathized with Fin.

"Besides, did you ever wonder what kind of things Derek is dealing with at home? Not all families have good mom and dads. Some parents don't treat their kids very nice. Maybe if you spent some time getting to know Derek's background and home life, you could have a better appreciation for why he is like that," his dad reported.

"Then you would also have more compassion for Derek as well," his mom responded.

Fin thought about it for a moment. Then a twinkle came in his eye.

"I think I might have a way to find out more about Derek without becoming his friend," Fin said beamingly.

"After supper, I think I will go outside to play for awhile."

Fin finished up his meal and headed outside to the snowman. He was going to take the snowman over to Derek's house and peer through the window to see what it was like for Derek at his house.

"Let covert op mission **INFO** begin," Fin said as he made his way to Derek's house.

CHAPTER 13

Covert Op Mission "Info"

Fin sneaked over to Derek's front yard in the snowman contraption. As he got closer to the front window, he could hear some arguing coming from inside the house. The voices became clearer as he got up to the front window. Fin stayed out of sight and listened.

"Can't you get this math right Derek?" a voice bellowed from the living room. It was Derek's father. He seemed to be pretty mad.

"We have paid a lot of money to get you a tutor for this stuff and you still come home with a "D" grade."

"Our money is being wasted if you aren't even going to try to improve," Derek's dad yelled as he threw the math quiz Derek wrote on the floor.

Finneus decided to peek into the window where Derek was. He could see a small tear coming down Derek's cheek as he felt the shame of disappointing his parents again. His father left the room and Derek was busy cleaning up the papers that were on the floor. Fin had never seen this side of Derek before.

"I guess dad was right," Fin said to himself. "Derek doesn't have a very good home life. I guess that's why he is always a bully. This is a really nice house, but after seeing this I'm realizing that I am truly the richer person."

Fin leaned in a little further and his carrot nose hit the window making a clinking sound. The noise caught Derek's attention and looked over to see the mechanical snowman peering at him through the window. At first, Derek had a bit of a frightened look on his face but it then drooped to an angered look stemming from the events that had just taken place with his dad. Fin knew he was in trouble now. Derek had the look like he was going to get to the bottom of this snowman mystery at all cost. Derek raced to the door to get his coat and boots on. Fin was frozen in fear for a couple of seconds wondering what would become of his safety if Derek caught him.

The door of the house broke open and out came Derek frantically looking to catch the snowman. Finneus broke out of his thoughts and put the snowman in full throttle. He sped away as Derek started chasing after him. The snowman was pretty fast but Derek was just that little bit faster than him. Fin had a good head start but Derek was slowly catching up to him.

Fin raced down the street and past his house to the field on the other side of the road. His Grandpa Joe had showed him this good hiding spot down by the wide creek on the far side of the field. They played there a lot in the summer and now, it was a place that Sarah and he spent time playing. Fin thought he could hide there until Derek lost hope of finding the snowman. Derek was inching closer as the chase continued. It seemed like the snowman was starting to run out of battery power just because Derek was coming and there seemed to be no chance of escaping. The snowman was still performing top notch though as they neared the far side of the field where the creek was. It was iced over by this time of year but the ice wasn't very thick.

Fin was warned by his parents not to go on the ice unless they were with him and said it was safe.

It seemed he would be trapped between thin ice and an angry Derek. Derek was only a couple of feet away from him now and closing in quickly.

Then Fin noticed the tree at the edge of the creek.

"If I can grab that tree with my snowman arms and swing around the tree, Derek might fall straight onto the ice and that will allow me to get away," Fin thought to himself. It looked like it was his only hope.

Derek was only inches away as the tree came near enough to grab onto. With one hand on the inside of the branch and the other on the trunk of the tree Fin managed to get a perfect swing motion around the other side.

Derek was not so lucky. He was so focused on trying to catch the snowman that he lunged at the snowman the same time that Fin swung the snowman around the tree. Derek had missed and had fallen onto the ice.

CRACK!, SPLASH!

Derek had broken through the ice. Fin didn't hear the splash as he was trying to get away as fast as possible. Derek wouldn't be able to catch up to him again. Then he heard this awful cry.

"HELP! I CAN'T GET OUT!"

Finneus stopped and looked back. There was no Derek chasing him. He heard the call again and thought he had better check it out. Fin wanted to be careful though for it might have been another one of Derek's tricks. He inched slowly over to the bank of the creek and looked over the edge of the small slope. Derek was there stuck in the ice calling for help. Fin was about to turn around and drive away when he heard His Grandpa Joe's voice speak to him in his head.

"Use your wisdom together with the goodness in your heart to help others. That is when greatness is attained."

Finneus knew the right thing to do was to help Derek even though he had been mean to him all these years. With a huge sigh, Finneus went back over to the tree he had just swung around. He grabbed onto one of the strong branches with one of the snowman arms and held out the other arm to reach for Derek saying,

"GRAB MY HAND. I WILL PULL YOU OUT."

CHAPTER 14

Surprise

"GIVE ME YOUR HAND!" Finneus said as he reached as far as he could. Derek hesitated just for a second but he knew he had to do something because there was nobody else around who could help. He held out his hand and grabbed for the fingers of the snowman. Finneus put the snowman in reverse and the track started to move backwards. There was a lot of strain on the motor as it was trying to pull out so much weight. Fin pulled with all his might. Grunting and groaning echoed through the air. One hand was on the tree and the other hand on Derek. Inch by inch Derek was gradually coming out of the freezing cold water. Fin could hear Derek strain as the coldness set in and his body started to become weaker. The battery in the snowman was starting to die as the final inches were passed and Derek was on the shore safely.

There was no hope for Fin now. There was not enough battery power left in the snowman to get away from Derek if he should start to come after him again. His only hope was that either Derek was too tired and Fin could get away by foot, or Derek appreciated his help and would stop doing mean things to him. Either way, Fin was going to have to show Derek who was in the snowman body. The rest was up to Derek. Fin decided he had better say a prayer in his predicament.

Fin prayed, "GOD, I know I haven't always made the best choices over the past few months. Please forgive me. I have to reveal who I am to Derek and I don't know how he is going to react. Please give him compassion and realize I used the snowman to help him in his time of need. I leave the outcome in your hands Lord. In Jesus' name I pray. Amen."

Derek lied lifeless on the snow beside the creek; too tired to move from the struggle getting out of the icy cold water. Slowly, he looked up and saw the snowman staring back at him.

"Thanks for saving me," Derek groaned as he struggled to get the words out. He was still tired but got to his feet.

His body was very cold and he needed to get some warmth soon.

"Who are you?" Derek squeaked.

Fin hesitated and then slowly got out of the back of the snowman and peeked around the back at Derek.

"It's me Derek," Fin replied with a small shaky voice.

Derek's eyes narrowed for a moment. Fin thought this would be the end of him for sure; but then something strange happened. Derek's eyes broke a small glistening tear. His narrow eyes opened and for the first time, Fin could see that Derek was not all bad after all. He actually looked thankful for the help he just received.

"This is the first time I can remember someone doing something nice for me," said Derek as he started to walk towards Fin.

Derek held out his hand to give Finneus a handshake. Finneus grabbed his hand with a hard grip to show that he was worth the trouble.

"You are welcome Derek," replied Fin.

"We had better get you to a warm place. You can come to my house to dry off and get warmed before you go home. I don't want you to get into trouble with your parents for being wet."

Derek smiled at Fin. They grabbed the battery out of the snowman to take home to be charged. Fin would have to come back another day with a charged battery to get his creation home.

They got back to Fin's house. Derek was really cold. His mom was waiting for Fin to get home. Carol was surprised to see Derek at her doorway all wet and cold.

"What happened to you?" Fin's mom asked Derek with a suspicious look on her face as she looked over at Fin.

"I fell into the creek across the field and Finneus helped pull me out," Derek stuttered to get the words out while shivering all over.

Carol's suspicious frown turned into a smile when Derek told her the answer.

"I have an old robe you can put on. Take your clothes off and put the robe on. You can sit by the wood fireplace to warm up while I dry your clothes," said Fin's mom beaming. She always loved helping others out.

Fin and Derek sat by the fire and stared at each other for a few minutes.

Would you like something to eat?" Fin said hesitantly.

"I'm sure we have some bologna you could have."

"Why are you being so kind to me?" Derek inquired.

"I have been mean to you all these years."

"My Grandpa Joe said that when I use my talents and gifts to help others, That's when I will achieve greatness. I finally realized that my snowman invention could be used for good instead of picking on you," Fin replied with somberness.

"You really got me good," smiled Derek.

How did you make that cool snowman anyway?"

Fin went on to discuss his invention that he was so passionate about. He also showed his electric garage door opener for the building block house. Derek watched with amazement as Fin explained all he was interested in. Derek spoke about some of his vacations too. They got to know each other pretty well.

Fin's parents smiled as they watched the boys become friends.

"Looks like it is time to give Fin the other letter from Grandpa Joe," Roger said to Carol.

"Yes, it appears Fin has reached the level of maturity far earlier than we had expected, but we had better wait until summer to give it to him," replied Carol.

They both looked at each other and smiled with pride as they realized they were doing a great job as parents of Fin.

Derek was finally getting warm enough to leave. His clothes were dry too.

"I had better get home," said Derek.

"I won't bully you anymore, but realize that I probably won't be hanging out with you either at school. I have a reputation to uphold."

Fin and Derek laughed and parted ways. Fin's plan had worked but not in the way he had expected. It appeared that love and kindness were the things Derek needed to change from being a bully to a respectable person; not to make him think he was going crazy.

CHAPTER 15

The Big Summer Adventure

Summer holidays were just about here. Derek lived up to his word. He didn't bother Fin the rest of the year. Derek still had his poor class of friends except for one. Fin was a secret part of Derek's circle of friends now. He would come over once in awhile to see what Fin had been working on and to learn what he could from him and his family. Derek was slow to change; but the change Fin and his family were seeing was a positive one.

Sarah hadn't changed. She was always finding a way to startle Fin or to play a harmless practical joke on him. The bond that Fin and her had was as strong as ever. They would probably spend almost everyday this summer having fun with each other's company.

It was the last day of school and everyone waved goodbye to Mrs. Black. Mrs. Black was always sad to see her students move on for they seemed to make an impact on her life. Students touched her heart in some way and she loved them all.

Finneus said goodbye to Sarah at her door and went off home to see his mom and dad. Fin had a little bounce in his step as he whistled the coat of many colors tune to himself as his mom always sang.

He arrived at his front door with his parents waiting for him at the front anticipating his arrival. Roger had taken off work early so that he could see Fin come home on his last day of school.

"Welcome home son," his dad said with excitement in his voice.

"Another year done," his mom concluded as a small tear came into her eye. To her Fin seemed to be growing up so fast, that she sometimes became overwhelmed with emotion.

His mom took Fin's backpack and set it in the house as they made their way into the kitchen. His mom had baked some cookies for Fin's last day as a surprise. Fin sat at his usual spot at the table and enjoyed the cookies in front of him.

"We have a surprise for you," said Roger as he was enjoying a cookie himself.

"Grandpa Joe had left us specific instructions not to give you this letter until we thought you were mature enough to receive it. We have had this for a while and have not read it. During the events that have happened with Derek this year, we decided that you have matured enough to read this," his dad spouted with joy.

Fin swallowed the cookie down hard and eagerly took the letter from his dad. He opened it up and read it aloud at the table.

> Fin. If you are reading this, then you have matured to becoming a great young man. I wanted to leave you with some things that will not only make you great, but make you successful as well. I have set up a quest for you to do as you have the time and desire to do it. Your first lesson is that anything worth striving for will take perseverance and good character.

If you should choose to accomplish these tasks, it will lead you to a treasure of ultimate wealth. There will be a number of clues to figure out. Feel free to use all the resources around you, (like the places we visited, the gifts you have received, and the people you know). This is your quest though. Make sure you are the one who makes all the final decisions on how to approach this quest.

The first clue is given on the next page. If you would like to achieve ultimate wealth then this quest will get you there.

Good luck Fin.

I have loved you always
Grandpa Joe.

"You guys haven't read this before?" Fin inquired as his face shone with excitement.

"No. We told Grandpa Joe we would not open it," his dad replied. Roger was getting excited too. He wanted to help. He was just as curious as Fin was about the treasure of ultimate wealth.

"What does the first clue say?" asked Carol.

Fin reached into the envelope and pulled out the second sheet of paper. He read it out loud again.

To get the next clue, you will have to figure out what to do.
Get rid of the glue to let the true color shine through.

"What do you suppose that means?" Fin asked.

"I'm not sure but I would be happy to help you with it," replied his dad with excitement.

"That would be great. If you think of anything let me know," said Fin.

"Grandpa said I was to be the person to figure these things out. I think I will go to Sarah's and talk to her about it."

His dad was hoping this would be a father / son adventure but respected Fin's decision.

"Let me know if you need any information about Grandpa," his dad responded.

Fin put the letters back into the envelopes and headed back to Sarah's house. He knocked on the front door of the house. The look on Fin's face was a sure giveaway that something was up.

Sarah opened the door.

"What are you so happy about?" Sarah expressed a confused look on her face.

Fin showed her the letter with excitement and Sarah read it. Her face turned as excited as Fin's.

"Looks like this is going to be the best summer ever," beamed Sarah.

How To Make A Snowman Mask

Materials:

1: Large Balloon

2: 2 Large Bowls

3: 1 cup of unbleached flour

4: 2 tablespoons of Salt

5: 4 ½ cups boiling water

6: White, Orange and black craft paint

7: White cotton balls

8: Newspaper

9: Cooking Spray

10: masking tape

11: toilet Paper role

12: seven marbles

13: white glue

14: string

15: Black See Through Material

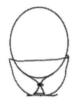

1: Blow up Balloon about the size of your head.
Tie off Balloon.
Place Balloon neck down in large bowl to hold.

2: Draw Line around Balloon with permanent marker as a guide for your mask.

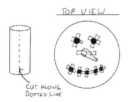

3: Cut toilet paper role lengthwise and roll into cone shape. Tape in place where nose should go on balloon.
Take seven marbles and tape them on balloon where eyes and mouth should go.

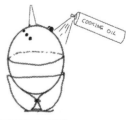

4: Cover entire working are of balloon with cooking spray.

67

5: In a large Mixing bowl, mix 1 cup
unbleached flour with
2 tablespoons of salt.
Pour in 4 1/2 cups of boiling water
and stir until the mixture becomes
like a paste texture. Add more flour or water
as needed to get the right texture.
Let cool before using.

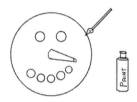

6: Tear newspaper into about 1 inch wide strips.
They should be about 6 to 8 inches long.
Tearing is better than using scissors.

7: Soak strips of newspaper in paste mixture
and place over snowman form above
the permanent marker line. Cover entire area
including the nose, but do not cover the mables.
Go around marbles. Let dry after each layer
3 layers total.

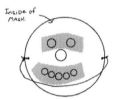

8: Remove marbles and paint the snowman
face white. Paint the nose orange and
put small black lines around nose
for detail. Let dry.

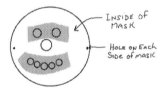

9: Glue some see through black material
to the inside of the mask with white glue.
Cover the eye and mouth holes with material.
Make a hole on each side of the mask to allow
for string to be tied around your head.

10: Tie a string in side holes of mask
at a length to fit firmly around your head.
Tie a knot in the string to secure it.

11: Paint white glue over all the white surfaces
on the front of the mask.
Be careful not to get glue on the nose, eyes or mouth.

12: Place cotton balls over all required glued areas.
Feel free to pull the cotton balls apart so
they look more even.

Enjoy!

About The Author

Kevin Watts is Thirty-eight years old. He resides in Waterloo, Ontario with his beautiful wife Lenora and his two wonderful boys Joshua and Brennan. Over the years, Kevin has entertained hundreds of children while performing magic shows, making balloon animals and drawing cartoons.

This is his first attempt at writing a novel. He continues to serve at his church regularly and desires to use his talents to touch others in a positive way.

I would like to take the opportunity to thank everyone who has taken an interest in my book. It touches my heart deeply to know that a common servant can have such an impact on so many people. May your lives be richly blessed by what you read and who you listen to.

My desire is that this is only the first of many novels to come. It would be a pleasure to write novels for both you and your family. I hope that these writings would encourage people generationally by brining families closer together.

God Bless